The Benefits
of Eating
White Folks

The Benefits
of Eating
White Folks

Leslie T. Grover

JADED IBIS PRESS

Grover, Leslie T.
The Benefits of Eating White Folks / Grover
Images by Lisa Teasley
Cover by Crystal J. Hairston

Published by Jaded Ibis Press.
http://www.jadedibispress.com

To my son, Ethan Grover, never forget that my love for you transcends all boundaries.

I

I tasted blood this time. The lash had sliced my face. I saw the Missus rear back again with the cedar branch, her lips pressed together in a thin line. I turned my head and tried to bury my face more deeply in the Whipping Ditch. But it wasn't enough. The branch broke, and she sent Jack for another one. I closed my eyes and inhaled the smell of the dirt, clovers, and blood. The Missus' foot came down on my stomach, knocking the wind out of me. Pain shot across my hips, and I reached to cover myself, but I felt shards digging into my skin. My hands and feet were swaddled with bug-lined cuckle rope. My wrists stung, and I tried to avoid my urge to raise my hands to cover my body again. Jack was back. I was afraid to open my eyes, so I asked God for this to be over, but I knew He could not hear my prayers above the sounds of the other ones I had already sent up to Heaven. They were too noisy in His Divine ears so He let me continue to suffer.

Divine Ears

Sometimes I wonder
If God exists for a Black woman.
If He does, He must not be good
At paying attention.
It has been well over
Two hundred years.
Maybe He is too busy
Watching the injustice,
Waiting to see if anyone
Is going to do anything about it.

eenie was missing. She did not run. She was not sold. She was not loaned out. She was missing. She was not dead. Nobody would even help look for her even though she was the Doctor's child. It was not a secret, and I was constantly punished for it. It was wrong to let her stay missing, and I tried not to say so to the Missus and the Doctor. I kept this to myself as long as I could. But I could not hold it in any longer. They looked at me with empty eyes and said maybe she would come back.

One of the Young Misters was sick, and the house was in an uproar. The Missus kept fainting, and the Brother's Wife kept calling for Old Sarah to bring them more blackberry lemonade. "Go get Young Sarah, Rose, and Addie. We need to see if all of us can figure out what to do," she motioned at Old Sarah. Old Sarah was sweating and she looked very tired.

Tears
· · · · · · · ·

I watch how the world laps up
White women's tears.
When she fucks up,
All she has to do
To get forgiveness
Is cry.

When we got in the house, we could see something was dreadfully wrong. The room reeked of hot vomit, which apparently was only the latest addition to whatever had been upchucked the night before. The Sound Young Mister was sprawled across his bed, breathing hard. He had crust around his mouth and his eyes were watering. I did not expect this to be the sick Young Mister. I looked at him as he lay limp on the bed trying to catch his breath. He closed his eyes tightly as though he were trying to will himself well. He was always stronger and faster than his brother. We called him Sound because even when he would fall off of his horse or hurt himself climbing trees, he would hop back up as though nothing happened. The Brother was taking the Sound Young Mister's pulse. He sent Rose to get water to wipe the boy's face.

The Benefits of Eating White Folks

The Other Young Mister was in the corner, comforting the Missus, begging her to sit up. "Please Mama, it is gonna be ok. It is likely something Old Sarah cooked. You know sometimes her food makes us feel funny. She makes too many greens. We don't like her greens." The boy was on his knees in front of his wilted mother. "My stomach is feeling funny too, and you know how sickly I am in the stomach." The Other Young Mister was right about this. Old Sarah's greens rarely sat right with either of the Young Misters.

Both the Other Young Mister and his brother had been sickly when they were Meenie's age, but the Other Young Mister seemed to get worse. While the Sound Young Mister had grown out of his sickness, the Other Young Mister often had trouble breathing in the spring when there was pollen, as though he were allergic to the spring season itself. With a snotty nose and red eyes, he would run in the house, leaving traces of his discomfort on the tables, the staircase, and once on Old Sarah herself when he sneezed directly in her face while groping her breasts. The boys were fourteen now, almost the same age as the Missus when she got seriously ill.

"He has a rash." The Brother pointed out the rash on the boy's lower leg. It was bright red, and it contrasted angrily against his skin. Nobody said anything, and the Sound Young Mister wretched and vomited again.

Addie and I started to clean up the mess, but the Doctor stopped us. "Addie, collect a sample for me. Young Sarah, get the women out of here so we can work." He looked at me. "Perpetua," he said, my name hanging bitterly in the air in front of him, "I have patients coming today. Make sure the infirmary is ready."

It was too hot for December. We always got an ice storm or some icy rain during this time of the year. But all we got this time was a lot of rain, humidity, and bugs. It was warm enough for the Young Misters to run outside barefoot, squishing their toes in the mud puddles between the pecan trees down by the Whipping Ditches.

The warm weather also brought a bounty of huge ink-colored blackberries that kept growing until the middle of December, like they were possessed by the Devil. The vines hung low to the ground, so low that the birds refused to eat them. These berries looked plump and sweet like the summer ones, but they were sour.

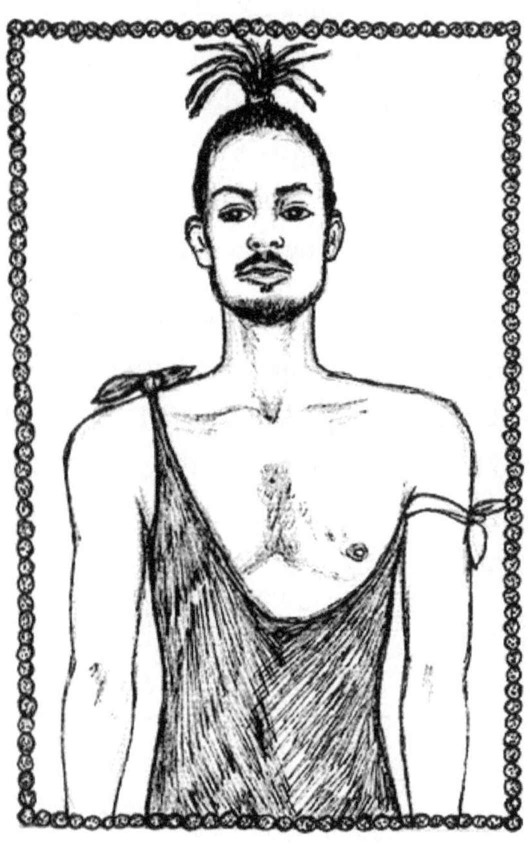

Leslie T. Grover

Sour
· · · · · · ·

The taste of justice has grown
Sour
In my mouth.
No longer will I utter it.
The quilt of waiting now smells
Sour
In my nostrils.
No longer will I cover myself with it.
The calls for peace sound
Sour
To my ears.
I will no longer listen to rhetoric.
The promises of allies are
Sour
On equity's shelf
I will no longer wait.

The Missus thought it was awful when the Young Misters gobbled those berries, grimacing and half spitting them out with a puft sound, making a mess in the kitchen. Still, she let them do what they pleased, as usual. She sat grimacing while the Sound Young Mister stood smashing the pufted out berries and leaving purple streaks all over the floor. Old Sarah and I looked at each other. Nobody could say a word to either Young Mister when the Missus was there.

With the weather so hot and damp, Old Sarah had to make lemonade for the Brother's Wife, to help with her warm spells. "Yours is the only one she can drink," the Missus bragged to Old Sarah as though this was a compliment. The truth was the Brother's Wife preferred bourbon to lemonade, and often she mixed the two when she thought no one was looking.

Old Sarah tried her best to prepare lemonade for the Doctor and his guests, but she was trapped in the kitchen. The Sound Young Mister slid across the floor on the sticky berry juice, stomping a few of the ones too soft for eating. It mixed with the mud from the puddles that was still on his feet, making a horrible sticky, slick mess. Old Sarah shooed him gently, and the Other Young Mister ran behind her, pinching her on her backside. He and his brother tormented Old Sarah, one pinching her behind and the other smearing blackberry mud. They only stopped when the Missus came to the kitchen to check on the lemonade, fussing at Old Sarah about her disrespect of the Doctor's friends.

The Missus and I had been friends since childhood. "We are just like sisters, except your hair will not lay down," she used to say, stroking my hair onto my face and trying to make sleek bangs like hers. "Maybe you should try to get your hair like mine," I would say, trying to get her hair to look coiled and strong. We would laugh, trying to style each other's hair and looking into each other's eyes. Like Mama's, my eyes were almost black, and they shone like silver pieces when I thought I was being clever.

When the Missus was five and I was six, they took me from Mama and sent me to live in the house while Mama lived in the quarters and in the field. She cried when I left, even though I was not going that far away. "Be careful not to be too pretty, child," she said, crying her tears onto the top of my head, as though baptizing me for safety. She pressed a small piece of stiff cloth into my hand. It was reddish-brown. "Keep this with you all the time. It will protect you. It was your Daddy's." The Missus' father had beaten Daddy to death for escaping to Panola County. I was four. I nodded and took the cloth, trying to remember Daddy as best I could.

Mama always said Daddy was good with his hands. He could carve anything out of wood. I could carve anything, too, and I carved figures and jewelry for the Missus and her friends. I even carved little deers in the Young Misters' beds and made them wooden soldiers.

I remembered all the times I saw Meenie playing with wood. I wished Daddy could have seen her, and I wondered if my mother had heard I had a daughter now, too.

I tried not to flinch this time. Another cedar branch splintered, leaving bruises on my skin. "Go get me the horse whip, Jack!" The Missus' voice sounded cold and squeaky, like wheels when they were about to break. I was still afraid to open my eyes or breathe too hard. I turned my head to the other side, and I was able to bury my face in my bonnet. It had almost come off my head.

When the Missus and I were younger, we used to go into public together, smiling. Her head was covered with a bonnet, and mine with the fabrics left from her dresses. Back then, we tried to match each other, but nobody seemed to notice our secret.

We had our forbidden secrets, too. When her tutor came, I always sat in with her on her lessons. I would listen to her recite and watch her practice her writing. The Missus was not much for schoolwork, except for drawing, so I would end up doing most of her handwriting work. I would read aloud to her and with her unfailing memory, she always fooled the tutor into believing she had done her studying between lessons. The Missus' father would always say, "You gonna let that little golliwog end up smarter than you. She ain't got the sense of a yard dog, and you ain't doing much better." She would laugh and kiss his cheek, and he would pat her on the head. When he left, we would dissolve into a puddle of giggles.

The Missus' father was a lawyer in the county. He and his wife Nan had just sold their place near the courthouse and moved closer to the river when the Missus first started her schooling. Nan was getting sick all the time, and they all thought keeping her near the river would do her some good. Nan loved the river, but it made her get worse. Her stomach swelled, and she said it was painful. Nothing worked to help her. She stayed vomiting up dark red sludge and soiling the bed with yellow muck until she finally died a few months later, convulsing and stinking up the room.

The Missus and Nan barely looked like they were kinfolks at all, let alone mother and daughter. While Nan was thin and pale with see-through eyes, the Missus was plump with dark brown hair and dark copper eyes.

The Missus got sick, too, shortly after Nan passed away, so she stopped her lessons. Everyone thought she was going to die as Nan had, soiling herself and retching in pain. The Missus was fifteen then.

She proved them wrong.

It was just after an ice storm that the Missus felt good enough to walk and eat a whole bowl of ground corn. I sat with her all day, holding her hand and wiping her forehead with ice water. I had to hold the bowl when she pissed or vomited. She upchucked blood. I always remembered how it smelled like metal.

When the blood started to dry on the Missus' bed clothes, it made me think of Mama crying and giving me that piece of rag, colored reddish-brown, like almost dried blood. I had known it was from Daddy before Mama even told me. She kept it stuffed in her bosom and she thought nobody knew, but everyone knew.

When Daddy was being carried away after they killed him, the rag he used to wipe his sweat fell from his corpse, and Mama picked it up. Mama cried every night when we went to bed, holding that rag to her nose.

Daddy
· · · · · · · · · ·

When I was born
My mama said I was so
Small
Daddy
Could hold me in the crook of his arm.
I saw a picture once,
There he sat in his recliner,
Arm stretched forward
With me swaddled and
Sleeping.

When I was a toddler
He told me his
Stories,
Speaking
Like they happened yesterday.
When he was my age,
His mother swept him up
And let white folks walk by
While they stood in the
Street.

Leslie T. Grover

When I was a teenager
My Daddy told me I didn't have to
Work
Only
Focus on my education.
That is how we break barriers,
Change the world,
And make the revolution
A reality for our
People.

When I got good and grown
My Daddy sat sickly
Watching
Me
Daughter, he said, *I am proud of you.*
I smiled at him and patted his hand.
Little did he know, I was
Only
Imitating him,
So I smiled and said
Nothing.

Even though Mama would whisper stories about how Daddy would never cry out when he was beaten and how he would always run off when he could, I could hardly remember Daddy's face other than his nose. I had his nose. Meenie had his nose, too, and his nature to fight. Even though she was only a little child, I could tell.

Because Meenie had the blood of Daddy, I knew one thing. I knew wherever she was, she was trying to find me, too. I thanked God for it.

Once we got grown, me and the Missus began to have different lives. For as long as I remembered, it was my job to go everywhere with her, help her bathe, clean up after her, and sometimes even take her whippings when she got in trouble. I often cooked for her and served her food. I emptied her slosh pot and cleaned the rags from her woman's time each month. But once me and the Missus came to live with the Doctor things changed.

The Missus married the Doctor a few days after she turned sixteen. The first few months, the Missus and I were happy. The Doctor often traveled to St. Louis while she and I stayed behind at the Big House.

Most of the Doctor's family had drowned in St. Louis when the river flooded in '44. His only living relative was the Brother who was caring for his own sick wife and their set of twin sons. The Missus told me the twins were kept in an institution because they were born simple.

The Doctor saw all types of patients and did everything from treating the Sickness to delivering babies in the cabins. One time he even delivered a baby in the field. The Brother, who was paler, fatter, and wore glasses, worked at a sanitarium in St. Louis.

The Doctor said he was a good doctor, but that he should step out and do "real work." The Brother mostly saw spoiled, fussy older women with fainting spells and plenty of money. But according to the Missus and the Brother's Wife, these women were victims of rascal husbands. Declaring them insane, their husbands had put them in the sanitarium. They took their inherited money and property and spent it all on whores or new, younger wives who could bear them children.

I guess the Sound Young Mister having the Sickness was the reason the Doctor wanted to start a hospital for children. The Sickness started out with just a few people who had traveled abroad, but then it continued to spread.

It started here with a few clerks in the court. Some of them had been working with his good friend, the Judge, and they came to the Doctor with vomiting and stomachaches. Some had rashes, so at first the Doctor thought it was just bug bites or that maybe they had picked up some parasites from traveling so long on the boats to Europe and India. But then fevers set in, and the symptoms got worse. Night terrors and visions of demons and fire tormented those stricken with the Sickness. They would scream and soil themselves and call out to Almighty God to help them. Within three weeks, they would be dead, eyes brown and glassed over with stickiness like burned sugar.

Sometimes the Sickness would go away for a while. Folks would actually feel better after three weeks. Their rashes would clear up and the vomiting would stop. Then, just when it seemed things were better, the visions would come back. The people would scream and their insides would churn loudly, sound like thunder. By the end of the day, the people would die the same way as before, eyes wide open and glazed over with brown stickiness.

The Sickness ran rampant with the white folks. None of us ever got it no matter how much vomit, piss, and soiling we touched. Often we would hear about how some of them would even apologize to God for all their sins. We laughed at how some of them pretended to love one another in church but hated each other everywhere else.

The Brother said the Sickness was going to run its course like most diseases. But then the white children started to get it and die.

It started in the Sunday school class. The Judge's boy threw up all over the benches and the shoes of the Sunday school teacher. The Young Misters and three other boys thought that was funny. They all laughed so hard that the teacher sent them outside until the morning service started. A week passed. The Judge sent for the Doctor, saying his son had a rash and kept screaming and pissing his bed from terrifying night visions. The end of the world is coming, the boy kept saying, and he would faint away again, slobbering and foaming at the mouth as his body lost consciousness.

The Doctor and the Brother went to help the boy. They treated him the best they could with tinctures and cool water, but he stayed throwing up and hallucinating. While the adults usually died within a month, the Judge's son lingered for a month and a half, feeling better enough some days to get out of bed and walk around. But that soon ended. They found him dead outside among the pecan trees, his eyes glazed over and sticky like the rest.

Sick

· · · · · ·

What will it take to admit
This place is sick?
Imagine how bad off
We must be to think
That being Black
Is enough for a
DEATH SENTENCE.
We can say what we want
But can we seriously believe
That people who have been
Beaten
Degraded
Oppressed
Lynched
Raped
Murdered
Will sit silently
FOREVER?
How sick is that?

The horse whip cut deeply into my chest when the Missus struck me. I heard myself yelp for the first time since she threw me into the Whipping Ditch. The petal from a spider lily flew into my mouth. Its bitterness mixed with the blood I had been swallowing. When the Doctor and the Missus got married and came to this place, the smell of cedar and river water and spider lilies was the first thing I noticed about the Big House. The smells perfumed the air everywhere, even in the kitchen. I had never smelled a place like that before. This spider lily in the Ditch was a surprise because I did not know where it came from. Jack sometimes had them tucked into his sleeves. Maybe it fell off of him when he went to get the horse whip.

The Doctor had a cook named Old Sarah, a groomsman named Jack, and three young women who worked in his surgery area, Young Sarah, Addie, and Rose. The Big House stretched long and flat with two stories. Hidden behind the

Big House, the Doctor kept a small office and surgery area with cramped living quarters. Young Sarah, Addie, and Rose lived there. Behind the Doctor's office and surgery, there was a covered well, a small cistern, and privies. A small stable with a few horses and the Doctor's coach sat near the privies. On the other side of the land behind the Big House, there was a cookhouse, a pantry, a smokehouse, a chicken house, and an icehouse that also sat near a covered well.

The Doctor owned a lot of land, but he had only a small vegetable garden and a pecan orchard. During the year all types of pear, plum, fig, persimmon, and apple trees hung heavy with fruit. Even when other trees around the county died or did not bear fruit some seasons, the Doctor's trees always did. Jack told me lots of folks respected the Doctor just because of those trees.

Young Sarah was Old Sarah's daughter, and Young Sarah sometimes helped with the work in the cookhouse. Addie and Rose hardly ever came to the house. I usually saw them when we all ate dinner at the end of the day. Only five of us consistently spent time in the Big House: me, Old Sarah, Addie, Young Sarah, and Jack.

I never talked that much to the Doctor. The only time he ever said more than two words to me was a few weeks after he and the Missus were married. "Do not ever go into my study, Perpetua." He said my name quickly, as though it tasted funny in his mouth.

Everyone said the same thing about that study, too. "He sure is funny about that study, and the only one who has ever been in there is Jack," Old Sarah said with a smirk during our dinner one evening. "But he ain't never gonna say what might be in there, though. Right Jack?" Young Sarah, Addie, Rose, and Old Sarah cackled, but I kept quiet and watched Jack. He kept his head down over his plate and poked at his food.

Praise The Lord Saints

Gentle Black Boy
No need to reveal
Your secret to me.
You are loved,
Even when you wear
Dresses and heels
Play with dolls
And wear lip gloss.
The preacher says
You will go to hell
But that will not stop him
From asking you to
Suck his dick.
Church ladies
Will giggle with you
But watch to see

If their husbands
Watch you when you
Walk by during the
Offering and altar call.
Keep your head high.
All of God's children
Matter and that includes
You and yours.
Remember one thing
When You are
Good and grown:
You are enough
To fill the spaces
Of anyone's
Joy in life.
Praise the Lord, Saints!

The Missus struck me again across my midsection. My stomach started to cramp. The pain was excruciating, and I knew I was losing the baby I was carrying. I had not started to show yet, but Old Sarah could just look at a woman and tell. Old Sarah knew a lot of things, but I had known that about her the first time I looked at her, way before I had any babies.

I did not know how old Old Sarah was, but her hair was completely white. Her skin was light, and she had one eye the color of leaves in the fall and one the color of the bark of pecan trees. She was short with an ample bosom, yet her hands seemed supernaturally large.

I thought of them massaging salve onto my cuts after being in the Whipping Ditch, warm and sure and comforting. I prayed again to God to help me as I heard the whistle of the whip going back through the air. The Missus wielded that whip with all of her strength. My stomach cramped again.

The Missus took a long time getting pregnant with the Young Misters. When she got pregnant with one baby, before we made it to the next spring, she had lost the baby, and then she was pregnant again. This baby did not hold, either. She lost it in the kitchen, crying out for me to help her. I ran to her, but it was too late. The baby arrived in a puddle of brown and red froth, bubbling and spreading out on the floor like a bucket of spilled blackberries.

It was fully grown, and its fingers and toes were shriveled and gray. It had a thick, cloudy looking gray film over its eyes and its blue lips were stretched thin as though it had tried to open its mouth and given up mid movement. It never took one breath.

The next year she lost another child, but this time the baby lived two days. On the day it died, it soiled its diaper bright green and stopped breathing. The Doctor and Addie worked for hours to get the baby to breathe, but they failed. The baby's toes were a deep purple color, and they curled under like dead leaves by the time they had finished. The Missus wept for a while, the circles under her eyes matching the color of the baby's toes. She cursed God for a few moments, then went to sleep, her knuckles white as she grasped the pillow to her chest. After she slept, the Doctor took her some bourbon. He had decided she should go to St. Louis for a few days to see a specialist.

The Benefits of Eating White Folks

The Missus had been gone three days when the Doctor pulled me into the forbidden study and shamed my body. He never said a word. He just grabbed me, pinned me down on the floor, and put himself inside me. It hurt at first, but he just kept violently pushing inside me with his hand over my mouth. His big hands pushed down onto my lips, making my teeth sink into the inside of my mouth.

I was afraid to swallow, so I choked and coughed into his hand. I tried not to whimper. It was getting harder and harder to breathe, and I hurt my throat trying to keep as quiet as I could. The way he groaned and pushed, I thought he was dying, but I learned later on that those sounds are part of getting shamed. I tried not to listen to his animal sounds.

From where I was pinned down, I surveyed the study, noticing what looked like hundreds of books, metal instruments, and a big desk. Papers with drawings on them were all over the floor. There was a couch and a few big, overstuffed lumpy looking chairs. There was a fireplace that looked barely used. It had papers in it, too.

The room smelled of mud, spider lilies, and bourbon. I felt blood in my mouth again, and this time I held my breath and prayed, Please God, if you hear me, let this be over. Finally, the Doctor finished. He shoved me out of his study and closed the door, wiping sweat from his face and looking as though he wanted to spit on me.

I did not know what to do.

I ran to the Missus' room and cleaned myself up. I stuffed strips of old rags into myself and washed my face and my hair. There was blood on my dress. I threw the dress in the fireplace, set it afire, and curled up on my pallet next to the Missus' empty bed.

I wished I could be a little girl again and be back with my mother, but I had no idea if she was even still alive. I thought about the rag she gave me when I was taken from her. I thought about Daddy's nose. I always kept the rag in my chest like I had seen my mother do. When I reached for it, I realized it was no longer there. I howled into my covers until I fell into a fitful sleep.

• 37 •

Broken Promises
· ·

I was never supposed to know

what such a horrid thing

looked like,

but I found the courage

to ask before

the shame sent

me

into blackness

red and pink

and yellow and white

swirled and

deadly

seems so innocent

against bright

blue

The Benefits of Eating White Folks

if only the sky
knew the promises it broke
with its beauty,
it would
weep
all the time,
but it does not give a
damn
if I live
one more day

The Doctor left for St. Louis the next day. The Missus and the Doctor stayed in St. Louis for almost two months. By the time they came back, I already knew I was pregnant because Old Sarah had told me.

She watched me as I ate my grits. "I made yours special. No eatin' out the big bowl for you, pet." She had mixed dirt and sweet potatoes into my grits, and she made sure I ate the gruel until I felt stuffed. "All of this will help the baby," she promised me. "I prayed over it, too, so the baby will avoid evil."

The Missus looked better when they came back. She hugged me and told me all about St. Louis, with its dress shops and shoes just like the ones in Paris. She told me about the boats and huge ships along the river, and the immigrants who sold the most delicious baked goods she had ever tasted. She talked and laughed without stopping for what seemed like hours. When she finally paused, she looked at me. "You look well, Perpetua. I can tell you have not missed your meals!" She started up again, telling me about how much she enjoyed a bubbling drink and how it made her nose burn.

As the days turned into weeks and the weeks into months, the Missus realized I was pregnant. She hugged me as we worked on our sewing together. "Well, I assume you and Jack like each other then?" Jack was tall with wide eyes and high cheekbones. His skin was perfect, with not a single blemish, and it reminded me of the color of wet pecan shells. Often I would admire him as he crushed pecan shells and mixed them into the soil whenever he planted new fruit trees or vegetables in the Doctor's small garden. Jack's body was lithe and strong, and he had the thickest black eyebrows I had ever seen. They matched his abundant beard. Surely he was a handsome man, but I never got the notion he was ever with a woman or sought to be with one. He spent most of his time working outside when he was not helping the Doctor, and sometimes he did house chores or helped the Doctor get dressed. Jack had been the Doctor's companion since both he and the Doctor were boys, like me and the Missus.

Addie and Rose once told me that Jack would remake their old dresses and keep some of them for himself. This struck me as funny because while Addie and Rose were both tall, they were both also much larger than Jack. Addie was buxom and had big hips and a big behind. Her legs reminded me of trees, and her feet were big and flat like the flounders we would sometimes catch in the river. She had a pretty face, and her coarse hair fell down to her calves when she took it down to wash it. It was as though God had taken all the cotton bolls out of the fields, painted them black, and put them lovingly on her head.

Rose, on the other hand, had no chest or behind at all. Instead, she was thin with narrow hips and strong legs. Though her skin was dark, red hair grew sparsely out of her head, as though it was afraid to be seen by the world. She had small feet and hands, and hardly any eyebrows at all. When she walked, sometimes, the wind would blow the back of her dress, accentuating her lack of a backside. "Nosatol," Old Sarah would giggle when she walked by the kitchen. "Whew, chile!"

I supposed Jack probably looked a lot better in Rose's dresses than in Addie's.

Leslie T. Grover

Whew Chile

· · · · · · · · · · · · · · · ·

God must have been feeling love
When He gave
The Black woman her laugh.
It sounds like
He mixed
The brightness of a sunny day
With
The warmth of the sun
And
The deepness of the ocean.
The sound is so beautiful
That when She
Exhales
Whew, Chile!
Maybe
God loses Himself
And
Falls in love with her
Laughter
All over again.

J ack did not say much to anyone. It was clear he had his own life. There were a few men like Jack in the county, and sometimes they met in secret. He had been caught one time wearing a dress, but it was not such a scandal since it was around the time of Fall Carnival. Often during that time, men wore dresses, and the children dressed up like cats and dogs. Jack almost got whipped to death, though, when he was found in bed with the Brother's houseboy during a trip to St. Louis one year.

Addie had once been to bed with Jack, she told me, but he could not make love with her because his manhood stayed soft. She asked him if he was scared and told him that it might help if he thought about Young Sarah. Jack laughed and asked how the thought of Young Sarah was supposed to help his manhood. I knew if Jack's manhood was still soft with the mention of Young Sarah that he certainly did not like women in bed. All men liked Young Sarah.

Young Sarah was not that tall, and she was not that short. She had yellow skin and light brown, curly hair that looked like earthworms to me. Her hair did not look regal and holy like Addie's cotton crown. Instead, Young Sarah's hair was more like the little dogs' the Missus and her sister carried in their laps to market or to the theater when they got baths. The strands seemed to stick together in some places, and some of the ends stood straight on end.

Young Sarah had a small waist, even without wearing underclothes. Her lips were full and pink, and anytime she smiled, everyone else in the room smiled, too. She did not get to go to town very often because sometimes folks thought she was white. White men would stare at her when she went to get soaps for the Missus or special instruments for the Doctor's office.

The Missus would be infuriated when this happened. She would cuss Young Sarah and chide her for being a whore. "No white man is ever going to stoop to the level of touching you," she would scream in Young Sarah's face. Young Sarah would keep her head down, smiling to herself. She was glad no white man would have her, and she refused offers from them all the time.

Thicc
· · · · · · · ·

This hourglass
Does not lie.
It tells every secret
I thought I'd hidden
Beneath this long dress.
It laughs loudly
At every joke
Stuffed into these
Jeans,
It jiggles an extra
Insult to Thinness.
It does not
Give
A fuck.

any had come to visit the Doctor, thinking Young Sarah was white. They asked for permission to court her. When they found out she was not a white woman, a few of them still asked to purchase her or for her hand in marriage, promising to take her to Mexico or Canada. Even the Judge asked that Young Sarah be wed to his groomsman, yet the Doctor refused.

Young Sarah was afraid of all men, white or otherwise.

She preferred to spend her days with me, Addie, and Rose. To keep down confusion, the Doctor confined her often to the small front room of the surgery. She worked with anyone who came to visit or had an appointment to get cut on by the Doctor. When men came, she scurried away from them, chattering quickly and making sure the Doctor could see them right away. She never went into town unless it was absolutely necessary.

I often caught the Sound Young Mister staring at her when he thought no one was paying attention. He looked her body up and down and gazed into her face, but she never noticed him. He even stared at her now that he was sick.

Still, no matter what anyone said, I liked Jack. He was gentle, and I liked the way he told me stories about his travels with the Doctor when he came to the cookhouse. The Missus smoothed my hair and patted my face. "If not Jack, then who?" I lowered my head. I tried to open my mouth, but my lips stuck together. "Pet, look at me." She lifted my chin with her finger and looked into my eyes.

We had always shared secrets, but I could not tell her the truth. "Pet, be honest"—she lowered her voice and almost whispered—"did you sneak off and fast away while we were gone?" I shook my head. My face was feeling hot and I felt a churning in my stomach.

"Was it one of the boys that comes here to send messages to my husband about sick people in the county?" Her eyes were big and inquisitive.

My shoulders felt heavy, like oak trees had taken root in them and were pulling me down to the earth. The Missus finally let go of my chin. I almost fell over. I prayed for real tree roots to spring up and take me down into the earth. The Missus sat quietly for a minute.

"Was it my husband?" Her voice was too still and too calm. I dropped my head again.

This time the Missus grabbed me by my hair. She looked into my eyes. Her face was drawn and her dark copper eyes seemed to turn a dull brownish-red, like the color of the bloody rag my mother had given me in memoriam to Daddy.

As her grimace grew into a snarl, she stared at me, and my eyes filled with hot tears.

My heart dropped into my stomach, and I knew this was not going to end well. I said another prayer in my head asking for the strength to withstand whatever was going to come next.

I had never seen the Missus look at me that way. I tried to lower my head again, but she grasped my hair tightly in her hand.

She twisted my hair. She was hurting me. "Answer me," she said, the words barely escaping the thin line of her lips. Her words sounded like a growl. "Perpetua, did you seduce my husband?"

I let out a deep sigh. "I did not want to. He grabbed me and took me into his study and then he got on top of me. My dress had blood on it. I—"

I was shocked into silence with a slap. The Missus' face was bright red. Never had she hit me, not ever in my entire life. When we were girls and I got a whipping, she would cry with me and rock me back and forth like a baby. If we went into town and a shop owner tried to push me or was mean to me, she would clear her throat and say, "I beg your pardon! She belongs to me, and you will respect her or we will not spend our money here!"

But we were not girls anymore, and she was not trying to protect me.

The Missus slapped me over and over again and I put my hands up to protect my face. She slapped and beat me until both of my ears felt full of water. She punched my face until I tasted blood in my mouth, and she strangled me with my bonnet until I saw bright white spots dancing in front of my eyes.

She grabbed me by my wrist and walked me outside to the Whipping Ditch beyond the pecan trees. On the way, she grabbed the rain stick I had carved for her as a wedding gift. She pushed me into the Ditch and beat me with the rain stick until it broke. Debris and small stones spilled from the stick all over me and into the grass in the Ditch.

She spit on me and walked away.

I lay in the ditch, quietly crying to myself and rolling around as though I were still trying to avoid her angry blows.

My friendship with the Missus was over.

The Benefits of Eating White Folks

Jennifer

When I was in fifth grade,
My best friend's name was Jennifer.
She had gray eyes
Freckles on her nose
And light brown curls, that made
Her look like Cupid.
We would talk on the phone
And laugh about
Boys we thought were cute.
Heath
Demarcus—
We had it all
Planned out.
We would live next
Door to each other
And our children would
Play together too.
The County Fair was coming
This weekend.

The Benefits of Eating White Folks

We should go together
And win prizes
Ride the biggest rides
And eat
Caramel popcorn.
But when I got there,
She was with two
White Girls
I did not know.
My mother told me
Never to go anywhere with
A Nigger,
She said.
And walked away
Leaving me
Alone
With the sick-sticky,
Sweet smell
Of popcorn.

I had trouble when the baby was born. Instead of the baby coming from between my legs, the Doctor had to cut the baby from me. The baby was small with six long fingers on each hand and seven toes on each foot. When it came into the world it did not cry. It screamed as though it was angry that it had come to the world this way.

Young Sarah said, "I am sad for you, Perpetua. Sad for this girl baby, too." But my baby did not live that long. She screeched all night, and died the next day, with her lips purple and her eyes yellow and filmed over like burnt cornbread. I was relieved.

I knew the Missus now hated me, yet I still held hope that she would take me back—that we could be friends again. But of course she did not take me back. She watched as the Doctor took the dead baby to his surgery. She did not say a word to me. She just huffed at me and patted her also pregnant stomach.

Nobody said anything to me for days after that, not even Old Sarah. She just gave me water with aloe in it and made me eat fruit. Healing was painful where the Doctor had cut me open to take out the baby. He stitched me with some thread and at night, it hurt and itched. Sometimes the incision would burn and I would hear the dead baby's incessant screeching.

I thought I was dying until one morning I woke up with the front part of my dress drenched. I was not sure exactly what was wrong until I realized my breasts were expressing milk. The Missus' baby would be coming soon, and I already knew I would be her wet nurse. I gathered up my sopping wet gown and went to ask Old Sarah what I should do.

The Missus gave me another lash with the horse whip, this time stinging the mound between my legs. I heard Young Sarah wailing, "Lord have mercy. Please have mercy." It sounded like she was whispering in my ear and yelling at the same time.

The Missus spoke again, but I could not understand what she said. There was a ringing in my ears and they felt like they were filling up with water.

I felt a plank being wedged between my head and my bound hands. I was pulled upright as the plank was put in the limbs of one of the pecan trees. My body felt heavy. It felt like the Whipping Ditch was holding me down in its trenches.

Pain rippled through my body, and I held back my urge to cry out. "God please. Please. Please," I whispered. I felt my bladder release. The wind blew across me. It made the muscles in my body ache and the piss on my legs feel cold.

It was windy the night before Meenie went missing. She had lain next to me, crying softly because one of the Young Misters had taken the toy deer I had carved for her. It was a tiny thing, but Meenie loved it. I kissed her hair and held her close. "I will make you another one," I promised her. She fell asleep after that, exhausted from her tears.

But then I realized her deer had not been taken at all. When I woke up the next morning, I found it on the table, right next to where Old Sarah usually put Meenie's breakfast. She was so happy that she grabbed it and hugged it to her chest.

Meenie did not cry when she was born. She did not make a sound. At first I thought she was dead like the others I had birthed, but she was far from dead. Maybe it was because Meenie was the only child that did not have to be cut from me.

She came easily, and it did not take long to push her out. The Doctor and the Missus had been away when she was born, and Old Sarah had helped me bring her into the world. As I labored, Young Sarah held me between her legs and told me to lean back and push. She sang and chanted in my ear, telling me to close my eyes. "Ase, Ase, the river flows. Ase, Ase." Old Sarah sang along with her, "Ase, Ase." I relaxed and leaned back, thinking of a flowing river that would take me away to somewhere peaceful, without a doctor who always shamed me in his study against the smell of sweat and spider lilies and bourbon. One who had left me stranded without my childhood friend and without anyone with whom I could share my secrets.

Old Sarah lifted Meenie to my chest. That child had the biggest, greenest eyes I had ever seen. Meenie looked into my eyes, smiled directly in my face, and passed gas loudly. We all busted out laughing. I sobbed a little bit, too, because I realized she had the Doctor's eyes, just like the Young Misters did. Those eyes were big and green and clear, and they could see right through to the center of the earth. Round and bucked, those eyes never missed a thing.

Meenie grew and grew and grew. Her skin was golden brown, tanned like the Italian women who sold hair bows and sweets in town. She developed into a solid child, tall for her age and strong, but she still had dainty features like a porcelain dolly. Every time I looked at her, I saw my mother, Daddy, and me reflected back at me. And while her eyes were the color of those of her half brothers' and her father's, she seemed more soulful in how she stared at me. This made her eyes seem darker in color.

Her eyes reacted to light as though she was about to smirk, squinty and turned up at the sides. It was like they had already seen all the secrets of the world and had laughed at them loudly in God's face. They glistened like my mother's; they held anger like my father's; and they observed the world like mine.

Meenie never crawled when she was a baby. One day when I was helping clean the surgery, she just stood up and wobbled over to me, her chubby fingers grasping the air. After that she just started walking as well as any grown person does right now.

If anybody noticed the resemblance between Meenie and her half brothers and father, nobody said anything. Even though I did not remember exactly what Daddy looked like, I wanted to believe she seemed more like him than anyone else.

She was strong for a girl, and sure enough, she could carry more wood and pick more blackberries than any of us. She loved working with wood, and she would bring me the most beautiful pieces so I could make things for her. The wood would be imperfect with notches or striations or it would be pieces of bark that looked like ghostly faces.

Even though the tree bark she brought me was not a good piece to carve, she insisted I make that deer for her out of it. I did not know why Meenie loved deer so much. We would sometimes see them around the Doctor's land. At night they would be near the pecan trees, or when it rained and the Whipping Ditch filled with water, they would drink from it.

The piece of bark she chose for her deer was brittle and it had small holes in it. It was thicker in the middle, and the ends of it crumbled as she gave it to me. But I carved a small deer from it anyway and she loved it. It was no bigger than a button. I took my time putting love into each cut, whittling away the brittle pieces and working mostly with the wood from the center portion of the bark.

When I was finished, she squealed and kissed the deer, gently rubbing its head. She talked to it as though it were alive, and slept with it in her hand. I do not know why it lasted and lasted through all her times of holding it tightly or getting it wet in the bath.

That missing deer is how I knew Meenie was truly missing. It's how I knew that the place she'd been taken to was close by or that someone she was familiar with had taken her away from me. Had she been snatched up quickly, that deer would still be here.

• 61 •

Gone

She stood on the porch
Her face
Contorting into
An ugly cry
When they told
Her the news.
But the cameraman
Did not cut away
And there was no
Station break.
Her bright green
Bonnet blew in the wind
And she crumpled
Off the porch
Onto the ground,
Losing one of
Her house-filthy slippers.

Her son was gone
And she could not understand
Why they would do
Such a thing.
He did not deserve
This.
Not.
This.
Not *this*.
She called out
His name.
Beat her fists
Into the ground.
But It Was
Too late.
He was
Gone.

When children were taken they were not able to take anything with them, not even the smallest thing. Taking mementos and personal items was too dangerous. If they took things with them, they might get too down and do bad work in their new places, or worse, they might try to find their way back home and get taken by hunters trying to make a quick dollar. Or they might be carried off into the woods by wild animals. That was why I knew my mother took a chance giving me the piece of the blood-soaked rag that had belonged to my father.

If Meenie had been taken, I would have found that deer by now. If she had been taken, Jack would have surely told me. Out of all of us, he was the one that got to drive to town and to talk to other families on other plantations. He always knew the latest news with the white folks, too.

Jack had not said one word to me about Meenie. Either way, she had been carried off by a human that wanted to take her someplace else. If they allowed her the pleasure of her deer, then they would not have killed her. She had to be alive still. I could feel her. I knew she was still alive.

Meenie was the only child of mine that had not been cut out of me and she was the only child of mine that lived. Old Sarah said it was because the Doctor himself was so evil.

"Tuh! I know white folks talk about those fruit trees, but that is because of Jack. Death follows that Doctor around like a trained puppy," she told me. "When he was a boy, he would steal plums off the trees and the trees would die overnight."

Old Sarah turned up her nose, "He would bring home birds with broken wings and fix them. They would die the next day. He would catch lightning bugs and crush them before they could shine in his hand."

Old Sarah breathed in, "When I got pregnant by his daddy with Young Sarah, I was tempted to let him touch me to loosen the baby from my womb"—her voice dropped off—"his own babies do not seem to want to live in the world because of him. Just look how they get crushed like those lightning bugs before their eyes even get a chance to shine."

A light flashed in my head. All the memories of pregnancies and beatings almost seemed like a distant dream. But right now was no dream. The Missus was still beating me, dust flying into the air. I tried to think back to something happy, but the thought of Meenie would not let me. The snap of the horse whip bit into my flesh, but the only true scarring was in my heart.

Again, the Missus raised the horse whip into the air with a *whrrrrrr* sound that made my heart feel as though it were about to come pounding out of my chest. The stinging lash brought tears to my eyes.

Please God. Let one of my prayers get through.

The last thing I remembered was the horse whip biting into the flesh on my chest. It hurt so much I could barely breathe.

I saw the blackness coming for me. I heard myself gasp for air, but my body rejected it. Maybe God had heard some of my prayers after all.

II

I decided not to say anything about Meenie, even when the Missus would try to get me to talk, and even if the need to say something about her burned a hole in my mouth. I had to be careful not to let anyone know I was trying to find Meenie, not even Old Sarah, Young Sarah, Addie, or Rose.

Whenever I thought of saying anything, I would go walking by the stables. The Missus was pregnant again, and the Doctor had purchased horses for the Young Misters to ride when the Sound Young Mister recovered. Even though he was getting sicker and sicker, he still had not had the hallucinations like the others with the Sickness. His sickness lasted much longer than three weeks. Yet he was not dead like the others.

The Missus and the Brother's Wife thought that was because he probably did not have the Sickness at all. However, the Doctor and the Brother insisted that he did.

They treated the boy every day with something they mixed up in the Doctor's back surgery room, and they said the more they learned from the Sound Young Mister's case, the better they got at keeping him alive.

The Doctor never let Rose or Addie mix the treatment and none of us knew anything about it. It was dark brown with flecks of black in it, and the Sound Young Mister had to drink cool water right after having it.

I knew it must taste bad because the Sound Young Mister had to be tied down and have his nose held and his mouth covered to stand it. He hacked and coughed and complained, but the Doctor and the Brother forced him to swallow it. Then the Doctor gave him an injection.

One of the horses was a deep sienna color. It reminded me of the sky when the sun was almost done setting. The reddish-orange coat shone so beautifully as it trotted alongside Jack the first day it arrived, that I gasped when I saw it. When I got up close to that horse, I could also see golden flecks in its coat.

As beautiful as that horse was, the other horse was my favorite. It made me think of Meenie. It was lower to the ground than the other horse, but I could see the power in its large body. Its mane was curly and short. Its coat reminded me of the way mud splattered on our dresses when we rode into town sometimes, the dirt randomly assigning itself spots and sometimes covering the hems completely. When

Meenie used to go with me into town, she would jump in the puddles and make the splatters even higher on her dress. Her eyes would dance with joy.

I knew one thing about that horse. It may not have been as majestic as the other one, but it was joyful and smart and curious. When Jack brought it back into the stable, it sniffed me and licked at my hands. I think me and that horse both knew at that moment that I would be sneaking back to pet it and give it things to eat when I could.

After my last whipping the Missus made me sleep on the back porch. Sleeping there was not so bad. It smelled better outside to me anyway, and when I could not sleep I could walk around the perimeter of the Big House and down to the stables.

Sometimes I could hear things going on, too. I knew when everyone woke up, and I could hear the things the Missus and the Brother's Wife talked about. I could hear the Brother humming hymns as he changed into his night clothes. I could hear the Young Misters talking to each other before they went to sleep.

The Sound Young Mister started having nightmares but refused to tell the Doctor so he would not have to be force fed more of the medicine. The Young Misters would take turns sleeping, so if the Sound Young Mister had a night-mare and yelled out, the Other Young Mister could awaken his sleeping brother from the dream.

The Sound Young Mister talked about dreams of being eaten alive by a big mouth in the back of the woods. He talked about pecan trees walking and chasing them, trying to stab them with their branches, and he talked about falling into the Whipping Ditch and being chewed up and swallowed, never to be seen again.

I heard everything, even the dreams about Young Sarah running naked.

It was safer for me to sleep on the porch, too. As much as I begged God to help me, I was pregnant again, and I had not lost the baby even after the Missus beat me with the horse whip. The evidence of her hatred now swelled into a thick line across my chest. But that is not the evidence I was worried about. I knew it would not be too long before I started to show. As usual, Old Sarah knew my condition before anyone else did, and she slipped me extra sweet potatoes after she closed down the kitchen.

Sometimes I saw the fireflies at night, lighting up like ancestors' eyes trying to watch me and see how I would live out my life. It was times like this I would pray to my mother, and wonder if she remembered me and longed for me, the same way I longed for Meenie.

Nights passed slowly, and sometimes, just for a moment, I had a glimpse of peace about Meenie. No matter what happened to me, I was never going to stop looking for her until I found her.

I prayed to God.

I prayed to the ancestors.

I prayed to my mother.

I even prayed to the lightning bugs.

Please tell me where she is, I begged them all. Please let her be ok. I begged them at night on the porch. I begged them in the morning when I worked. It seemed like all I did was beg, and the only thing that came back to me in my spirit was to do one thing: listen.

That is exactly how I found out there were children, like Meenie, missing from other places. The Doctor was talking to one of the overseers who worked on the other side of the county. We often passed that place when we rode into town. It was not as big as the Doctor's land, but it had acres and acres of cotton, pear trees, and goobers.

The man had come early one morning when only Old Sarah was awake preparing for the day's meals. Jack had to go awaken the Doctor because the man threatened to wake up the entire house if he did not hurry up and get the Doctor.

"Now, git on Nigger, I ain't got all day. There are children getting sick!" He shoved Jack so hard that he tripped backwards.

His ears bright red with rage, the Doctor was still dressed in his night clothes when he let the man into the house. He and the man spoke in violent whispers in the study. I was not supposed to be up, so I crouched down by the study's window listening as hard as I could.

"There are many others," he said to the Doctor, "and you need to come see what is going on. I ain't gonna keep calling you." The man slammed the door of the study when he left and stomped out the front of the house. I watched him mount his horse. He was short and stocky and his muscles seemed too big for his frame. His skin was burned reddish-pink and scaly from the sun. He spit and then drove his heels violently into his horse as he rode away.

The Rebuke

· · · · · · · · · · · · · · · ·

How dare you fix your mouth
To call me out of my name,
Out of my character
Out of my natural form!
I am the Divine who,
In my love for your sorry ass,
Allowed you to be blessed
By my presence.
The lips you part to spew
Hot words
Are the same ones that
Kissed me below my dreams
until my hopes jerked

That hummed sweet lies
Of equality in my ears
Of promises to my heart—
Of sweetness to my soul.
Say it one more time
And I will come down
Off my throne
Make a bolt of lightning
Tie it to your
Own words
And
REBUKE YOU

The Doctor was still in the study with his head in his hands. Jack had told us that more and more white children in the county were falling ill with the Sickness. While a few had already died there were still a great many who were having symptoms. More seemed to be getting sick by the day. Everyone in the county was depending on the Doctor and the Brother to make it right. But the Doctor was spending his time trying to keep the Sound Young Mister alive.

The boy was still very ill, but he was alive. Many of the county folks knew this, and they felt the Doctor was keeping secrets. After all, it had been more than three weeks, and the Sound Young Mister outlived everyone who had suffered from the Sickness. The Doctor had even missed going to church, sending the Brother and his wife along with the Missus and the Other Young Mister. Rose, Addie, and Young Sarah heard the white folks talking.

I did not always understand the things white folks did, but I knew the love they must feel for their children, like we do. Jack had told us that the only children who seemed to be getting the Sickness were white children. No slave child seemed to be bothered by it. He said the Doctor and the Brother often talked about why this was the case.

The Doctor thought it was because white children's superior systems made them react more quickly to maladies. A quick reacting system often experienced more sickness, but that is because the brain worked so quickly and efficiently in white children. Our children simply didn't have quick minds so diseases traveled slowly and had time to take root and be killed by organisms in our blood.

The Brother thought it was because white children and our children had to have physical differences that had not yet been discovered. His theory was that as we age, our bodies become more alike. He said Black bodies were more like horses in childhood because we rarely felt pain and worked too sluggishly to ever keep anything in our bodies other than a cold from time to time. "The biggest worry for them," he said, "is trying to be smart enough to avoid getting a beating or getting worked to death."

I thought about the spotted horse in the stable. I knew that horse was safe from being worked to death because Jack would teach the Young Misters to ride horses, and never would he be so cruel as to abuse any living thing, not even a horse.

Jack had taught us all to ride horses. "Do not be in a hurry at first," he kept saying. "Let the horse take its time and learn to trust you. And you take time and learn to trust it. It takes both of you working together. Easy, easy."

I crept back to the porch and rolled up my pallet. Tonight, I planned to start looking for Meenie. Had the Doctor sold her to that overseer? Had the Missus sent her away to St. Louis? Was she somewhere suffering or being worked to death like a horse? Maybe everyone was just pretending they did not know where she was.

I needed to help Old Sarah freshen the water for the house, so I gathered a few pitchers and bowls and headed to the well. Jack was there with tears in his eyes. He had pissed his pants, and when he saw me, he hid his face.

"I sat down here to pray to see what God would say," he was sobbing to me in a throaty whisper. "Now you have come here and I have my answer."

He got up and walked toward the back of the property. In all my time living at the Big House, I had never been to the back of the property. I am not sure why, but it always seemed forbidden. My stomach felt like lead as he walked in front of me. Not only was it full of briar patches and snakes, but behind it was some woods. I was sure a river was beyond that, but my mind stopped there.

I was distracted by a cramp in my stomach. I quickly pushed the discomfort to the back of my mind and focused on Jack who was walking in front of me.

As we walked all I could think about was Meenie and the baby inside me making the walk more and more difficult. Finally the cramping stopped, and Jack did too. I looked up and realized I was near some briar patches at the end of the Doctor's property.

We often picked blackberries on the other side of the Doctor's land, closer to the Whipping Ditch, but never had any of us come this far. I did not know there were blackberries on this side of the trees. All I knew was that there, in the midst of some briar bushes, was what appeared to be what was left of a small girl. My stomach cramped again. I burped loudly and hot vomit spewed from my mouth before I knew it.

I stared at the girl.

Her body was strewn facedown among the briars, the girl's coiled, dark brown hair spread out like a riding cape around her shoulders. One of her arms was tucked under her, and the other was extended into a clenched fist. The back of her fist had a cut on it, but the cut was clean. There was no blood anywhere.

There was pee all over the romper she was wearing. It had begun to dry in a yellow stain on her clothing. I recognized the clothing immediately. The outfit was one of the ones I made for Meenie. I knew it was because it was made from some scraps of dresses from the Missus and the Brother's

Wife. My stomach lurched again and this time I gagged. I had pieced together whatever was left from the dresses. The bodice was pink with small green and gray flowers, and the ruffles on the bottom of the legs and the sleeves were white with little embroidered leaves. Meenie had worn it only a few times because it seemed to be too big.

The Missus hated it when she saw it. She turned up her nose, "She is dressed like a circus clown, Perpetua." She narrowed her eyes and continued snarling at me, "Maybe I should sell her to one of the shows."

My head was too heavy to hold on my shoulders. I was on the ground on my knees and before I knew it, I was eye level with the soles of the little girl's feet. Her heels were smooth, and the bottoms of both her feet supernaturally white as though they glowed at night. The romper was tattered at the bottom. The thorns were holding her body there, a deformed crucifixion in the briar patch.

Jack put his hand on my shoulder. "We need to turn her over."

"Wait, Jack. We need to see what that is in her hand." I steadied myself and reached for her hand, but I drew it back to my stomach, which was cramping almost unbearably. I doubled over and took a few deep breaths. Dear God, I tried to pray. But another cramp came and knocked the wind out of me.

"Let me." Jack took a handkerchief from his pocket and

used it to open the small fist. Inside of the child's hand was a small piece of cork.

He turned her over.

Her face was small and angular with thin lips and small eyes. The front of the romper was drenched in more pee, and I could see some of her insides had escaped into the vines of the briar patch.

I dropped forward onto the ground, losing control of my bladder. My abdomen felt heavy again, and I wretched.

This girl was not Meenie.

The Missus was angry with Jack, but she could not do anything to him because of the Doctor. When we came to live with the Doctor, he told the Missus that Old Sarah, Young Sarah, Addie, Rose, and Jack were all passed down from his family and that they must never be harmed. Never had they been beaten or mistreated, and never would they be. He often chided her when she yelled too loudly at Jack. Aside from the Brother, they were all he had left of his family. As heirlooms they were meant to be spared many of the horrors and mistreatment others faced.

The Missus did not do anything to Jack's body but she did yell at him and cuss him and talk to him like he was simple.

"Stop acting weak and do as I say!" My bonnet had been removed, and I was kneeling in the Whipping Ditch. "I said hold her head still!"

Young Sarah and Rose stood with their hands over their mouths. Jack knelt beside me. He put one hand on top of my head and another on the back of my neck. Jack's hands were soft and with him so near me, I smelled his spider lily scent mixing with his sweat.

The Missus put the branding iron in the fire that had been built under the pecan trees. Jack passed gas and started to sob.

Meenie did not like spider lilies. She always said they smelled like crying. I wondered what she meant by that, but now I understood. At every funeral we ever had, there were spider lilies. There was always the heat of tears and sadness.

There was a funeral for the little girl we found. She was the child of one of the women at a plantation on the other side of the briar patch. Jack and I went to pay our respects.

The girl was laid to rest in a small, wooden box. They buried her behind one of the houses in the quarter, which we assumed was her family's house. All the women wailed and cried. They called out to God asking why. The men stood silent and tall, looking like trees, their hands hanging helplessly at their sides.

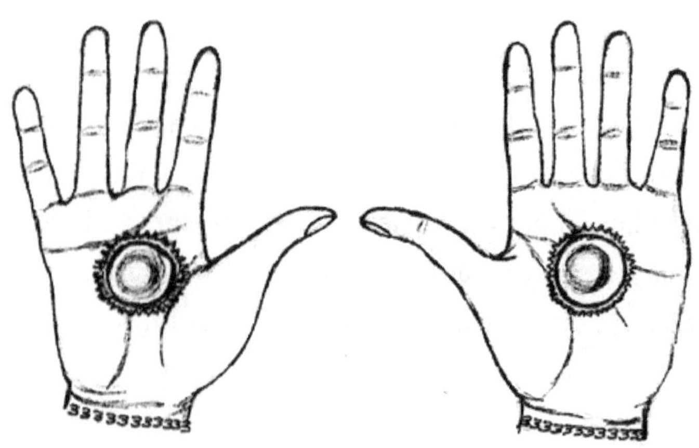

Leslie T. Grover

Hands

Surely the ancestors feel my love
When I grasp these masters
Of love,
Of support,
Of pleasure,
In mine.
They raise their hands in praise
In worship
In horror
In celebration
In submission
To Blackness.
We must cover ourselves with them,
The ancestors remind me,
Protect them and
Tell their stories.
Ase.

The death of one of our children did not mean much to the white folks, but to us it did.

Neither the Doctor nor the Missus would have officially let us go to a funeral, but since Jack was able to come and go as he pleased most of the time, it was no problem for him. County folks were used to seeing him around by himself, and he knew folks on just about all the plantations in the county.

Surely it was a problem for me. The Sound Young Mister was still as sick as ever, and I was supposed to take turns with Addie, Rose, and Young Sarah looking after him and cleaning up his vomit and his mess. I left the funeral early to make sure I made it back before anyone realized I was missing.

Even though I walked back quickly, the walk still took longer than I expected. The sun was going down, and it felt like the earth was trying to pull me down by the hairs between my legs.

I knew I was losing this baby, too, but I refused to give that process my time. I was glad to lose this baby anyway. All the babies just added to the hatred the Missus carried for me in her heart.

Instead I wondered how the little girl had gotten the clothes I had made for Meenie. Could the Missus have given them away? Did she give them to Jack to take away? Was Meenie at that plantation? Had Jack been secretly taking clothing to her there?

Children all over the county were dying. The white ones from the Sickness and ours from something else. Nevertheless I knew Meenie was still alive. I could feel it buzzing in my bones like mosquitoes in the night. I closed my eyes and imagined her face. I prayed for her protection. I prayed for her return.

Please God.

Please Mama.

Please Daddy.

ack yelped but the Missus ignored him. She held the iron in the fire while staring at me. For a minute, I thought she was going to change her mind, but she did not.

She put the branding iron near my face. I could feel the heat of it as the Missus drew it near me. I closed my eyes, preparing for her to burn my face.

The singe came quickly, except the Missus pushed the iron into the space between my neck and my shoulder.

It did not hurt at first, and for a moment it even made me feel relieved. When she pulled back the iron, I could smell my cooked flesh.

It smelled like burnt corn.

Jack's hands were shaking. My head felt heavy, and the branding was beginning to burn white hot. The Missus put the branding iron back into the fire.

Fullness filled my ears. Please, God, let this be over.

I let myself rest for a minute. I tried to prepare myself for whatever the Missus had next for me. I raised my head and looked directly into her eyes. She stood frozen, staring at my face.

Even though I was losing the baby, I went back to the plantation where we had the funeral, sneaking along the edge of the backwoods and the briar patches.

I took one of Old Sarah's big knives with me, thinking I could cut through the thicket, but it was hard to see at night. I hewed a small hole for me to climb through, but my dress and bonnet still ripped.

The other plantation was more segregated than the Doctor's. At the back, next to the thicket, was the fresh grave of the child we buried earlier.

In front of the grave site were the quarters. There were eight houses, and they all seemed too still in the night. I listened to see if I could hear stirring or talking, like I did at the Doctor's place, but I heard nothing.

"Please God," I whispered, "show me the right house." I knocked quietly on one of the doors.

"Who be there?" It was a woman's voice.

"Perpetua from the Doctor's place. I need help." My whispers sounded loud and hollow in the night. Crickets chirped loudly as though they were announcing my arrival to the entire quarter. I stopped myself from shushing them.

The woman opened her door. I could see children asleep on the floor. A man was draped on a large straw bed. The man slept soundly.

One of the children, a small boy with big eyes, sat up and looked at me. His eyes looked blue in the moonlit house. The woman kissed the boy on the head, and closed the door behind her. She looked me up and down as we stood face-to-face on the porch.

"You running north?" She sounded scared.

"No, I want to know whose baby that was."

I could see tears welling up in her eyes in the moonlight. "Why?" She wiped her nose.

I tried again. "Did you know children were missing from other places around here?" She seemed older than I was but not by much.

"Yes, we all know about that," she sniffed.

"The overseer from the place over on the other side of the county came to visit us, and he said there were white children sick there," I offered up this information to her.

"We know that, too. They say the white people are eating up our children. Putting them in stews."

She stared at me. I could see her clearly in the moonlight. She was brown, like me. Two braids hung below her bonnet. She was smaller than I was, but she had large breasts that sat like two round stones in her nightdress. We stood quietly for a moment. I felt lightheaded and my stomach cramped again.

"They did not eat the little girl we found. Who did she belong to?"

"What does it matter who she belonged to?" The woman raised her voice. "She dead ain't she? She belongs to God."

Another cramp wracked my body, and I stumbled back and almost fell off the porch. The woman with the braids caught my arm and sat me down gently. "You are losing that baby. Let me go get you some help." I kneeled on the porch, looking up at the bright moon, listening to the crickets chirp. I wondered how she could tell I was pregnant, but that did not matter anymore.

The pain was beginning to become unbearable. I thought of Meenie, and I hoped she was asleep by now. I felt so tired. I let myself be pulled lower and lower down onto the warm boards of the porch.

I could hear crickets chirping loudly below the boards, as though they were singing just for me. I wanted to close my eyes and listen to them, but I dared not. I had to keep my eyes open. I had to watch and listen in case Meenie was somewhere around here.

The woman seemed to be gone for ages. All I could do was pray and try to keep my eyes open. The burn on my neck was throbbing, and soon it mixed in with the pain in my stomach.

Finally, the woman with the braids arrived with two other women. They helped me walk to another house. The house smelled like smoke and spider lilies. They took me to a small back room with a large straw bed. There was a small window, where the moonlight shone in. A tattered quilt was at the foot of the bed, and once the woman with the braids lit a torch, I could see it had the same patterns my mother used to tell me stories about.

One of the patterns looked like two curls back-to-back. I thought hard, back to when I was little, about what my mother had taught me about those symbols. It meant strength. I would have to have strength right now, and as much as I wanted to close my eyes, I would not. I could not.

My stomach cramped and heaved again. I saw flashes of white light in front of my eyes like lightning that had lost its way traveling back up to the sky in search of a storm.

Those flashes were lost, just like Meenie. I felt myself closing my eyes, so I tried to count the flashes. I had to focus.

One.

Two.

Three.

Four.

The women put me down on the bed and gave me a bitter drink.

Five.

I gagged as I drank it. It tasted like grass and dirt and the sour blackberries with their ink juice. It made me feel like I needed to vomit.

Six.

Seven.

I heaved and my body convulsed. My abdomen jerked violently. My back arched toward the ceiling as though God Himself had a string and was going to pull me up by my belly, through the roof, up through the skies and right into heaven. I resisted.

Eight.

Nine.

Ten.

Eleven.

I was not going anywhere without Meenie, not even to see God Himself. Please, I begged Him in my head, let me stay until I find Meenie.

Twelve.

Thirteen.

Please God if she is here, let me find her.

As the jerks began to tamp down, I realized I had been holding my breath. I forced myself to exhale. I felt a clump slide between my legs. The lost lightning stopped flashing. If it had found its way to the storm it had gotten lost from, then Meenie would find her way back to me.

One of the women patted me on the head. She loosened my bonnet and stood over me. Her face was large and round, and her hair hung in three braids down her shoulders. She smelled like spider lilies. She smiled, revealing a wide gap between her two front teeth. In the light, I could see she was light-skinned, almost white, with dark eyes. Her face looked strong and muscular, and I could see she had a long neck.

"You passed the baby," she whispered, "but we have to take the rest out of you." She positioned herself behind me, her legs spread. Pulling me back onto her belly, she held my shoulders firmly back, wrapping her arms around me.

I knew this part was going to hurt because Old Sarah had taken me through this routine many, many times. The woman with the braids held my hand. "Try not to push and try not to draw up," she said softly.

The second woman, an older brown-skinned woman with a full face, reached inside me and pulled. I yelled out, not because I was in pain, but because I felt something cold inside me. The woman's ample face was smooth except for deep wrinkles in the corner of her eyes. She peered into my face, and I could see she favored my mother.

This lady was shapely like my mother, and though she did not have muscles like the light-skinned woman, I could tell she was strong.

The coldness got worse inside me as the full-faced woman twisted her arm and pulled again. I felt another cramp, and I closed my eyes. Pain shot through my body like lightning. I thought of my mother again.

The gap-toothed woman made me feel at ease as she hummed and pulled me upward so the full-faced woman could put her hand in me and pull more from my abdomen. I wished for a moment that she were my mother, but my mother would have been much older than this woman was by now.

The full-faced woman rubbed my stomach with her other hand, pushing down. I felt pressure there, as though I needed to pass gas. I felt my body tighten.

"I almost got it all, baby. Just try to be still."

Try To Be Still

Try to be still
When they murder
Your children.
When they re-enslave
Your men.
When they take
Your stillborn baby,
Leaving a streak
Of blood down
To your navel.
When they blame
You for where you live.
You won't get the mortgage loan
But you can get this
Part-time shift
That won't pay enough
For you to buy lunch
On your break.
You won't get justice
But you can get

The Benefits of Eating White Folks

This ugly ass
Birkin bag that your
Favorite Insta-ho
Says is all the rage.
All the rage?
Baby you are
All the rage!
But try to be still
When they tell you
That you aren't
Enough,
But congratulate
That Trashian white
Chick for her new BBL
And her next
Kid,
Still out of wedlock.
Meanwhile these
Diors take six of
Your part-time
Checks.
But try to be still.

She pushed down again. This time I felt all of her weight on me. I felt my insides jerk and then came more pain. This time instead of throbbing cool pain, the pain was warm. It radiated between my legs and settled heavily in the small of my back. The gap-toothed woman held me tightly.

The full-faced woman twisted and pulled one more time and the warm feeling melted away. Searing heat took its place. Above me the moonlight seemed to get brighter and whiter through the small window.

I tried not to move, so I focused on the moon as the pain spread through my body, willing it to show me where Meenie was. Shine on her brightly, I commanded it. Let her know she is loved and missed and that I am going to find her. Let her know her mother will never leave her or allow her to be away from her again. Let her know that after this, no matter what happens, that her life is going to be one free of her body getting shamed.

Let her know she is going to be free of the Whipping Ditch.

I asked God to please make the moon obey me. Please God, if you only hear one word of this prayer, let it be about Meenie. I held these words in my mouth and stored them in the back of my throat.

I made a pact with God then and there that if Meenie would just be okay, that if these women could just help me that I would give my life for Meenie. The Missus could take me to the Whipping Ditch every day if she wanted to, just as long as Meenie could come back to me. Tears streamed down my face, and I gasped as the full-faced woman removed her hand from inside me and left the room.

The gap-toothed woman unwound herself from around me, and the woman with the braids put a cool towel on my head and made me finish the bitter drink. The gap-toothed woman stuffed me with wet rags and let me lay quietly for a while. I could hear the full-faced woman and the gap-toothed woman talking among themselves in the front part of the house.

"She is not going to be able to have any more babies," I heard one of them say. "Part of her womb came out when I pulled out the rest of the baby. That baby had some of the womb in its hand and in its mouth."

"Will a baby eat its own mother?"

"Never seen that before. Are you sure it was the womb in the mouth?"

I heard a woman sigh deeply. "Look at what she passed." There was shuffling and more movement. "See? There is a film over the eyes. Even though it is little, you can still see it. And look at those hands. It still has some of the womb in it."

"I have never seen a film over a baby's eyes like this."

"Maybe it was supposed to be a veil."

"I do not think we should let her see it. We should burn it and tell her the baby was born dead."

"It is her baby, either way."

"What if she done brought the Devil here with us? Our children already—"

"Hush now! The baby just had something wrong with it! God knows what He is doing. He is in control and no evil can win against His will. And I do not think she is evil. The mark was on the baby but not on her. And we know how she caught this baby."

Leslie T. Grover

God Knows What He's Doing

Why is it when something awful happens,
Old Black people say
God knows what He's doing?
It's not like He's the one
Who killed Black children or
Lynched Black men in the streets.
God knows what He's doing
They say.
But
He doesn't kill young people
Who only want to escape from poverty.
And He doesn't
Grant favors to addicts with hearts busted open.
Why should God
Get all the credit for knowing
Everything,
When we're the ones
Who have to
Fix
His
Mess?

The gap-toothed woman stayed with me. She removed the cool towel on my forehead and began rubbing my legs and my back with something that smelled like anise. "Please," I begged her. "Whose baby did they bury?"

"Why do you want to know?" I could feel my legs and hips relaxing as she rubbed in the salve. The heat and the pain were both easing up.

"Because my baby is missing," I spat out the words I had been holding in. "I have to find her some kind of way." My insides ached and felt cool again. I closed my eyes, anticipating more pain but it never came.

The woman stopped rubbing me and wiped her hands on her dress. "I rubbed you down in some goldenrod. We can hide you here for a while so you can sleep, but you have to be gone before morning. Right now you can do nothing about finding your child. Just try to rest and stop talking and thinking about her."

The other woman came back from the porch. The gap-toothed woman looked at me and shook her head while the full-faced woman offered me an apple. She patted my hair. "Your baby died. It had something wrong with its eyes. There was this film over it. I do not think it would have lived anyway. God knows best sometimes."

She turned on her heel and walked away.

The gap-toothed woman stared at me a moment and then left the room, too. Tears welled in my eyes. I wanted to believe God knew best. There was no way He would allow me to be treated so kindly by these people if there was not a reason. He would not let me come to this place if He did not mean for them to help me, even if it was in a small way. Please, God, let them know something about Meenie.

My head felt hot. I sat up and looked directly into the face of the woman with the braids. I put my hand on hers and tried to raise up a little in the bed. "I need to find my girl, and I need to know whose baby it was that was killed. She looked so much like my child. I thought it was my child. Please. If I can talk to that girl's mother I can see how my girl may have come up missing. I need to know—"

The woman with the braids patted my hair and squeezed my hand. She pushed me gently back down. She gave me a little more of the bitter drink.

"Take a few bites of the apple," she said. "You will feel

better." I started to protest but she pushed the apple into my face and refused to move it.

I bit into the apple. It was tart at first but then sweetened as I chewed it more. Until that moment I had not realized how hungry I was.

The other women returned with water. "Drink this," the gap-toothed woman said. Her hand was shaking as she pushed a small cup of water into my hands. "You ain't gonna catch no more babies. This baby latched on to your womb and refused to let go."

I gulped the water. It was cold, and as I swallowed it, I could feel my chest expanding. Had I been holding my breath again? I inhaled and exhaled just to remind myself to breathe.

The gap-toothed woman pushed gently on my stomach and felt around. I felt gas getting ready to pass, so I tensed up. "Relax yourself." She pressed down harder, and I finally passed gas. "I think your womb is closed now. As long as it does not rot, you will feel better."

She kept pressing a bit more. I did not pass any more gas. I did feel better already though. The aching inside me felt cold now, but I knew I could walk. "I thank you all for helping me." The women looked back and forth among each other, giving amused side eyes. "If ever you need anything, please let me know."

I tried to stand, but fell back down to the bed, heavy,

as though someone punched me in the stomach. My neck throbbed angrily now, as though making up for being outdone by the pain of losing the baby. In my painful losing of the Doctor's baby, I had forgotten all about my neck. It throbbed and sent shivers down my spine. I winced.

The full-faced woman kneeled beside me and held my hand. "God we come to you humble as we know how asking for protection over this child of yours. We are all your children and your daughter needs you right now. Give her strength to do your will and ease her mind so she can understand your ways and your plan. Take away anything evil that may be on her, inside of her, or in front of her and add in everything good. Protect her. Protect us. Amen."

The moonlight was bright as the full-faced woman smiled on me. "No need to talk for now," she said. "Rest a while and eat the rest of the apple. We will wake you when it is safe for you to go."

The full-faced woman and the woman with the braids left the room. The gap-toothed woman took one of the rags she had with her and put it on my neck. She rubbed goldenrod into the aching brand there. "Rest."

There were no more hot and cold jolts of excruciating pain and even my neck seemed to hurt a little bit less. Even though I needed to talk to the woman of the buried child, I was worn out. The sounds of the night seemed to be closing in around me. I listened as crickets chirped. Please let God have heard our prayers for removing evil.

I closed my eyes for just a minute. Maybe I would rest here like they said and ask them about Meenie when I woke up. It seemed like I had only closed my eyes a minute before the woman from the porch shook me awake.

"You need to be headed back now." She helped me sit up, and wiped my face with a warm rag. She secured my bonnet on my head and placed another apple in my hand. She helped me sit on the edge of the bed and then to stand slowly.

This time I was able to stand with ease, but I knew walking home was going to be hard. "I can walk you as far as the wall of briars, but after that you will have to make the rest on your own. Do you think you can make it?"

I nodded. I would have to make it.

As we walked, I thought I would take a different approach to the subject of Meenie. I slowed my pace and looked directly into her eyes when we got close to the place where we would have to part ways.

"Was the baby who was killed yours?" I searched her face. Even if she lied to me, I would be able to see the truth in her eyes. I took her hand in mine.

She lowered her head and took a deep breath. "The dead child was not mine. My child was killed a few months back." She snatched her hand away from me and covered her face. "My child was a boy, and like yours his father is—"

I patted her shoulders. I knew what she meant. Her child, like mine, had been fathered by the man who owned her. "You do not have to say," I told her. "How did your baby go missing?"

"I woke up one morning and he was gone. That was it. Nothing. I do not know what else I can tell you."

"Did anything happen the days before? Did anybody say anything to you? Was he a good child like mine?"

The woman from the porch smiled. "My Mathias was more than good. He was sweet, smart, and a perfectly delightful child."

"So is my Meenie. I am sorry about your baby."

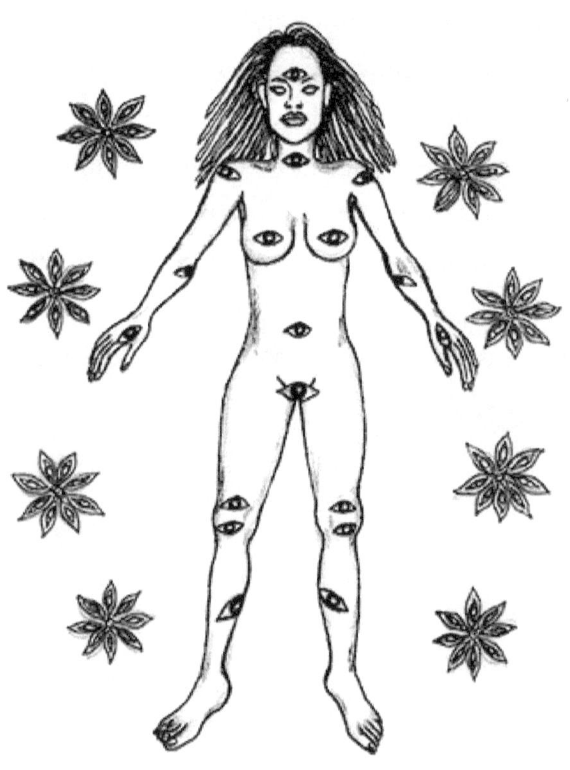

I Am Sorry About Your Baby

I am sorry about your baby.
I cannot imagine how much he meant,
He was the best part of you
And yet the world will never see him.
I am sorry about your baby.
Perhaps she could have been the one
To lead our people to the real Promised Land.
And all you got were broken promises.
I am sorry about your baby.
Add this to the list of pain—
Your body keeps score.
Loss: 1
Life: 0
I am sorry about your baby.
Maybe next time you
Will give birth to a Revolution
To heal our sorrows.

"You said your name is Perpetua. Mine is Easter. Try not to worry about your baby. As long as you have not found a body, everything will be ok."

"When Meenie came up missing, it broke my heart. But I know she is still alive. I just need to know where she is so I can make her safe again."

"The children in the Big House here have the Sickness. Your Doctor came and they are not any better, but they are not any worse either."

"The Sickness is in our house, too," I looked at the sky, and I knew I would need to get going if I were going to make it back to the porch in time to avoid being found out.

"I know the Sickness is at your house. The white folks here talk about it and wonder what is going on in that house"—she dropped her head—"I did not have a chance to miss my boy. We found his body in almost the same place we did the other child."

"Thank you, Easter, I—"

"You need to go. Be careful going back." She hurried back toward the quarters.

She did not look back.

IV

Months passed. I sometimes sent messages to Easter and the other women, but each time Jack returned, there was nothing from them. I thought of them every time I touched the brand on my neck. It had caused me so much pain before, but now I traced its softness and fatness with my fingers to comfort myself. None of us knew what it was or what it meant, but I could feel its shape. It moved up then dipped sharply then it went up again at an angle before finally going straight down again.

The Sound Young Mister was unbelievably still alive. Whatever the Doctor and the Brother were doing with their work, it was showing improvement, but only in the fact that the Sound Young Mister was still alive. By now all the other white children in the county were dead, all except the Sound Young Mister and the Other Young Mister. The Doctor and the Brother treated the white children the best they could, but eventually the progress they made went away. They all still died, living out false dreams and shitting themselves into oblivion. Yet the Sound Young Mister and the Other Young Mister lived. Only I was not sure what that actually meant.

The Sound Young Mister was always a muscular and sturdy boy, but now he was drawn and lithe. Their whites now yellow and streaked with flecks of red blood, his green eyes almost sat outside of his face, bulging and glassy. His piss smelled of burnt wood, and nothing he ate ever came out solid.

When he talked, his breath stank up the room. It reminded me of the rotted innards of horses that Jack sometimes had to bury when a foal died. I thought of the horses that had grown beautiful and strong in the stables. The sienna horse had grown even more beautiful, and the golden flecks in its coat glimmered in the sun and almost seemed to shine at night. Jack had told me that my favorite, the mud-flecked one, was actually a mare. She was even stronger now, and could run faster than any horse Jack had ever trained. The Other Young Mister was riding both of them now. He broke his little finger when my favorite threw him after he lashed her too hard. I never got the chance to go and feed her for her good deed.

The Sound Young Mister's sight was failing too. He was almost blind in one eye, yet the other eye was unaffected.

Of course he apparently did not have any problems with his sight when it came to mischief. Each morning when Old Sarah went to his room to take him breakfast, he would weakly pinch her bottom.

Still alive.

At one time, the other white folks blamed the Doctor and the Brother for their deaths, but now they had moved on to something else. There was political talk about a war possibly brewing, but no one was really giving it much thought. Surely our country would not turn on itself and fight with itself! Still, in the midst of all the political talk, white folks kept dying and the children the Masters had with some of us kept coming up missing.

Jack only seemed to be the bearer of bad news these days. As much as I loved him, each time he came with news, it was always about another child like mine going missing. It was to the point that I could always tell when he had heard or seen bad news.

Another child had been found.

I prayed all the time now, begging God to let me find Meenie. I knew she was still alive. I could feel it, but now I felt something else. There are not any words to say exactly what it was I felt, but my heart knew something else.

"Perpetua," he said to me after dinner, "go see Easter tonight. She wants to meet you by the cabins." We sat quietly and I looked at him. His eyes were red, and I knew he had been crying.

By the time I made it to Easter's cabin, the night was dark. She sat on the edge of her porch, her braids hanging limply beneath her bonnet. I could hear her man snoring inside.

"I am glad you came back to see me. I need to tell you a story." I looked at Easter. Her face was drawn, and her eyes were cast downward as she spoke. "I still remember my grandmother before I came to this place. She was from Sierra Leone, and she told me to never trust white folks no matter what they say or do, even if my life depended on it.

"I always listened to her and believed everything she told me. I believed her when she told me about white people, but this was not about my life. It was about my child's. Mathias." She sniffed, fighting back tears.

"I never knew my mother. She was beaten to death short-ly after I was born because her master was jealous." Easter touched her braids. "I wear my hair like this because my grandmother used to. Her braids were long, down to her waist. She was proud of her hair. It was soft like clouds, and I used to play in it when I was allowed to sleep with her. She told me that my mother's hair had been exactly like hers.

"She worked in the house most of the time, but after I was born she was never allowed in the house again. My grand-mother said I was with her the day she was killed, but I do not remember any of that.

"The Sickness came to this house early. Your Doctor and

the Brother came here to tend to the sick. I heard the white folks talking. That Doctor was the only one who could help folks."

I was anxious to hear what Easter had to say, but I wanted her to get to the point. I knew she did not call me all this way just to tell me a story. There had to be something else. I breathed in deeply and held my peace. I did not want her to shut down or change her mind.

"Do you know what the Doctor does to help with the Sickness, Perpetua?"

"No," I said trying to keep my voice from wavering. My heart was in my throat and I was starting to feel like I was about to pass out. I knew something was not right, but I could not place my finger on it.

"Children," she said quietly. "They use children."

"What do you mean, Easter?" I was starting to feel sick. My stomach lurched into my throat. "Do you know where my Meenie is?"

Easter's body drooped over as she sat on the porch. She began to cry softly, rocking back and forth with her arms wrapped around herself.

"Children like ours helped them treat white folks with the Sickness. They would take all of their blood and mix it into elixirs for sick white folks. That is what happened to my child even though they promised it would not happen to mine. Not my child." She let out a deep breath and tried to stop crying, but she was overcome again. I watched as her shoulders shook with grief.

"Grandmother told me not to trust them. She said not to trust them," Easter continued. "My child was taken in the night. I never ever saw her again. They fooled me. I never had a choice at all. When my master's children fell sick, and the Doctor and his Brother showed up, I knew something was wrong.

"They gave me that bed for my cabin, and they let me keep my other child with me instead of sending him to the fields. They even gave me clothes for Mathias. They brought him such nice clothes. Then he was gone, just like that. The children got better for a while, but they eventually died.

"The girl in the woods was not mine. Her name was Dorcas, and she was my sister's child. When the Master's Wife got sick, they took Dorcas. They brought your Meenie's clothes for Dorcas. Then she was gone." Easter began to cry again.

"Do you know where Meenie is, Easter?" Easter did not look me in my eyes, and she did not stop crying. I moved closer to her, and hugged her as she wept. Her body was hot from her tears. Her body felt like dead weight on mine as she shook and cried and tried to breathe.

Gasping for air, she gained control of herself. She swallowed some air and burped. Breathing deeply, she ignored my question and continued her story. "Your Meenie is not here anymore, Perpetua. Do you understand that she is the reason the Doctor and the Brother took our children?"

I stared at her.

"When they took Dorcas, my sister decided to run away. But before she did, she went to the Big House and tried to steal a few things for money. They caught her before she left the Big House. She was dead before the end of the day.

"My grandmother said white folks never should have stayed in the world this long. All they do is lie and steal and take for themselves. They break promises and make plans. They took our children."

Finally she composed herself enough to stop sobbing. Easter stood up and smoothed her skirts. She looked at me, grimacing. She said quietly, "Perpetua, they took Meenie first. Your Meenie is like Dorcas, Mathias, and all the others that have gone missing to keep white folks alive. We should never trust them. All they do is take from us. My grandmother says there are no benefits on earth from white folks. When we first came in contact with them we should have eaten them."

I did not say anything to Easter. I felt my legs push the rest of my body up. I walked through the night, numb.

All my mind could think of was the benefits of eating white folks.

The Benefits Of Eating
. . . .
White Folks
. . . .

What are the benefits of eating white folks?
Not white as in skin
Or white as in color
But white as in White?
Maybe we should have eaten them
The first day they came to Africa,
Enamored with Her riches.
Instead of wooing Her to give,
They raped Her and refused to use
Oil to ease Her pain.
What are the benefits of eating white folks?
Not white as in skin
Or white as in color
But white as in White?
Maybe we should have eaten them
The first time they said
A Nigger should do the work
I am too lazy or stupid to do.
They got rich and
All they did was
Sit on their asses

Leslie T. Grover

And steal a whole America.
What are the benefits of eating white folks?
Not white as in skin
Or white as in color
But white as in White?
Maybe we should have eaten them
When they said we were all free
But still built cages to keep us in
While we do their work and
Suckle their children.
What are the benefits of eating white folks?
Not white as in skin
Or white as in color
But white as in White?
Maybe we should have eaten them
When they bombed our buildings.
Seems like all they do
Is kill when they have a bad day
Even little Black girls in church
Or blonde toddlers in kindergarten.
What are the benefits of eating white folks?
Not white as in skin
Or white as in color
But white as in White?
Maybe we should eat them.

When I got back to the porch, Jack was waiting for me. I looked him up and down.

"Did you know about this, Jack? Is Easter telling the truth? Did you know?"

Jack lowered his head. "Perpetua, I did not know until Easter told me. But everything makes sense."

I pushed past Jack and into the kitchen. I grabbed a knife, walked into the Sound Young Mister's room. His skin glowed white as the moonlight bathed it. He was breathing through his mouth, and I could smell his breath. I put the knife to his throat trying to find the courage to slit it.

I closed my eyes, and in one sweeping motion, I did it. A wave of red blood spilled down the front of his night dress. He grabbed at his throat as he gurgled more blood.

I felt Jack's hand around my waist. He pulled me back from the sleeping child, back to the porch.

Meenie was missing. She did not run. She was not sold. She was not loaned out. She was missing. She was not dead. Nobody would even help look for her even though she was the Doctor's child. It was not a secret and I was constantly punished for it. It was wrong to let her stay missing, and I tried not to say so to the Missus and the Doctor. I kept this to myself as long as I could. But I could not hold it in any longer. They looked at me with empty eyes and said maybe she would come back. Now, I knew that since she would not come back to me, I must go to her.

Acknowledgments

I want to first give thanks to the ancestors who suffered, fought, and sent inspiration to me.

Thank you for allowing me to write stories and tell truths through fiction. I honor you in these words and remember your resilience.

Mama and Daddy, thank you for your sacrifices, hard work, and most of all, your love. Without you neither this book or I would be here. You're my most immediate ancestors, and because of you, I grew up thinking nothing was out of reach. This book is the manifestation of your amazing parenting and most of all your love.

Reginald, my brother, thank you for never giving my love for writing a second thought. Thank you for making it so normal and ordinary that I could do nothing else but follow my passion.

To Nikol Andersen who read and encouraged me and who made me feel like I was a true writer. I often prayed for a sister when I was young. Never did I think I would have one who would come into my life and become truer than blood could ever imagine. Thank you for reading, laughing, editing, and boosting my head up, even though you're far from a sea witch.

To Allison Bonner Shillingford—a true mentor, friend, and all around amazing person—thank you for helping me

along the way with advice, the power of story, and for believing in me. When I doubted you said simply, "When a
story is finished that's all there is." You never allowed me to
give up on the writer I was afraid of. She lives and you res-
urrected her!